CONTENTS

CRUNCH

Lisa Trumbauer

illustrated by Sean Tiffany

Librarian Reviewer
Chris Kreie, Media Specialist

Reading Consultant
Mary Evenson, Teacher

www.raintreepublishers.co.uk
Visit our website to find out
more information about
Raintree books.

To order:
☎ Phone 0845 6044371
🖨 Fax +44 (0) 1865 312263
🖥 Email myorders@capstonepub.co.uk

Customers from outside the UK please telephone +44 1865 312262

Raintree is an imprint of Capstone Global Library Limited, a company
incorporated in England and Wales having its registered office at 7 Pilgrim
Street, London, EC4V 6LB – Registered company number: 6695582

Edited in the UK by Catherine Veitch
Creative Director: Heather Kindseth
Graphic Designer: Hilary Wacholz
Originated by Capstone Global Library
Printed and bound in China by Leo Paper Products Ltd

ISBN 978 1406213 80 5 (hardback)
14 13 12 11 10
10 9 8 7 6 5 4 3 2 1

ISBN 978 1406214 01 7 (paperback)
14 13 12 11
10 9 8 7 6 5 4 3 2

British Library Cataloguing in Publication Data
Trumbauer, Lisa, 1963-
Pit crew crunch. -- (Sport stories)
813.6-dc22
A full catalogue record for this book is available from the British Library.

CHAPTER 1

THE CONTEST

As soon as he got home from school, Daniel ran to the letterbox. He flipped open the white metal lid and carefully slid out the post.

Nothing. Still no letter from the NASCAR officials.

While flipping through a magazine the month before, Daniel had seen an interesting ad. The ad announced a new NASCAR contest.

The winner would be able to work on a pit crew for one of the major race car drivers of NASCAR! All Daniel had to do was write a short essay, fill out some information, and send in his entry.

Daniel couldn't believe his luck. He loved NASCAR more than anything. Winning the contest would be a dream come true.

He knew a lot of kids would enter. But he thought he had a good chance anyway, since he loved NASCAR so much.

He'd given it his best try. He had filled out the form straight away and sent it in that very same day.

I think NASCAR is the best sport around! Daniel had written. *You have to know how to handle a car. You have to understand engines, tyres, and tracks.*

NASCAR is more than just knowing the rules. It's about knowing the mechanics of cars and racing, too.

With my love for cars and racing, I think I'd be an excellent member of any pit crew.

It wasn't hard to explain why he loved NASCAR. The hard part was waiting to find out if he'd won. What was taking the selection committee so long to make a decision?

Daniel went back to the house. He kicked the gravel on the drive.

He'd been so certain that the notice would come today. After all, it had been almost a month since he sent in the form.

As he walked up the front steps of his house, he heard the phone ring. Daniel ran inside and answered it.

"Is this Mr Daniel Granger?" asked a man's voice.

Daniel clutched the receiver. "Um, yes. Yes, it is!" he said.

"Mr Granger, this is Lee Harlow at NASCAR headquarters," the man said. "We are pleased to announce that your contest entry was one of only a few chosen out of several thousands."

Daniel gulped. "It was?" he asked.

"Yes!" Mr Harlow said. "You may be able to work in a pit crew during a NASCAR race!"

CHAPTER 2

TESTS

Daniel couldn't believe it. He'd actually won the contest! "That's amazing!" he told Mr Harlow.

"I'm sorry it took us so long to call you and tell you that you'd won," Mr Harlow said. "I hope it was worth the wait!"

"It definitely was!" Daniel said.

"Good. I'll be sending you some forms to sign. I'll also send you some information about NASCAR," Mr Harlow said.

"Information?" Daniel repeated. "But I already know pretty much everything about NASCAR."

"Yes, but there are rules about working in the pit crew," Mr. Harlow explained. "We can't just let anyone behind the scenes of a NASCAR race. You'll have to pass a few tests before you can help out."

Daniel hadn't thought of that. "So it will be a while before I'll actually work on the pit crew," he said.

"Not too long," Mr Harlow said. "Take a look at the information I'm sending and see what you think."

Daniel didn't need to look at the information to decide. He knew he'd do whatever it took to be able to work on the pit crew.

He'd dreamed of being part of a NASCAR race for his whole life. He wasn't going to mess up this chance.

After Daniel hung up the phone, he called his best friend, Josh. Josh was just as excited about the pit crew spot as Daniel. Daniel told him everything Mr Harlow had said.

"What do you think the tests will be about?" Josh asked.

"I have no idea, but I'm sure I can pass them, whatever they are," Daniel said. "Will you help me out?"

"Of course," said Josh. "But I don't think you need to worry. You know more about NASCAR than anybody, except maybe your dad. You'll definitely pass the tests."

* * *

Another week went by. Daniel checked the post every day. Finally, there was a thick envelope from Mr Harlow inside the letterbox.

The envelope contained some forms for Daniel and his dad to sign. Mr Harlow had also sent a lot of information about NASCAR and about working on a pit crew. Daniel read all of the information really carefully.

The biggest problem Daniel knew he had was that he'd never worked on a real car before. The pit crew preferred members who were experienced. Working on the crew was not easy.

Daniel knew it would take practice and hard work. He wasn't afraid of that. He was just worried that he didn't have the right skills to join the crew.

He'd won the contest, but that didn't guarantee him a spot in the pit crew. He hadn't realized when he entered the NASCAR contest that he'd have to pass so many tests.

"I wonder how many more kids have been chosen," Daniel said to Josh.

"Why don't you call Mr Harlow," Josh suggested. "I bet he could tell you."

"That's a great idea!" Daniel said. He found Mr Harlow's phone number and rang him.

Mr Harlow answered the phone straight away. He told Daniel that four other people had been chosen as possible candidates for joining the pit crew. They all needed to go to the racetrack in two weeks to take the tests.

"I really want the spot, Mr Harlow," Daniel said.

"I like your eagerness, Daniel. Just be prepared when you come to the racetrack," Mr Harlow told him. "We'll see then if you've got what it takes."

CHAPTER 3

HELP FROM DAD

On Sunday, Daniel and his dad planned to watch a NASCAR race together. Daniel loved watching the races and hanging out with his dad. It would be the perfect time to tell his dad about the contest.

Just before the race began, Daniel brought all of the information from Mr Harlow into the living room. His father was sitting down with a bowl of crisps and some lemonade, getting ready to watch the race.

"Hey, Dad, look at this," said Daniel. He handed his father a copy of the essay he'd written about NASCAR.

"Is this for school?" Dad asked.

"No," said Daniel. "It's for NASCAR."

"NASCAR?" his dad repeated. He looked puzzled and read the essay.

Daniel explained how he had entered the contest. "Four other people won, besides me," he said. "Now I have to pass a test to be on the pit crew. So what do you think, Dad?"

"Well, I'm not sure," his father said.

Daniel took a deep breath. He remembered what Mr Harlow had said on the phone. Daniel needed to show that he could be a great pit crew member.

"I was wondering if maybe you could help me," Daniel said. "I need to learn how to change tyres and jack up the car. And maybe you could show me how to quickly screw in the lug nuts and stuff."

"So if you pass the tests, then you get to join the NASCAR pit crew?" his father asked.

"That's what Mr Harlow told me," Daniel said. "He said to meet him next Saturday at the track here in town."

Daniel's dad was silent for a moment. The only sound in the room came from the NASCAR commentator on the TV.

Finally, Dad said, "It sounds like a great opportunity."

Daniel was once again afraid to breathe. "And?" he said.

"And I think you should definitely go for it," his father said.

"All right!" Daniel said. He pumped the air with his fist.

"This is going to be a lot of hard work," his father said. "None of it is going to be easy."

"I'm ready for it!" Daniel said. "I feel like I've been ready my entire life!"

"Okay then," his father said. "Let's take notes during this race. Then we'll go out to the garage. We'll see what you can learn on my car."

Then Daniel and his father watched the NASCAR race. Together, they paid close attention to the pit crew. In fact, they watched the pit crew more than they watched the cars!

They looked at the second hand on the wall clock in the living room. They timed how long the pit crew took to change tyres, tighten nuts, and jack up the car to look for damage. It only took the crew a few seconds to do all of that work.

Daniel felt nervous, watching the pit crew fly through their tasks. How could he ever work that fast?

That week, with his father's help, Daniel learned how to change a flat tyre. His father timed him as Daniel jacked up the car and loosened the lug nuts.

They went to the gas station. There, they timed how quickly Daniel could inflate tyres.

By the end of the week, Daniel felt like he was ready. He was ready to face his competition.

* * *

On Saturday, Dad and Josh went to the track with him.

When they arrived, Daniel looked around. Some other boys were there, talking about the contest.

Daniel guessed that they were the other NASCAR fans who had won the essay contest. He hadn't expected all of the other winners to be so much older. They were also a lot bigger.

Daniel felt like a little kid compared to the other boys. His confidence drained away.

CHAPTER 4

NOT SO BAD

"Daniel, did this contest have an age requirement?" Daniel's dad asked.

"It said thirteen and up," Daniel said. "I thought a lot of other thirteen-year-old boys like me would enter too."

"Do you recognize any of these guys?" Dad asked.

Daniel shrugged. "No. They must be in high school," he said.

"In what grade? Fifteenth?" Dad joked.

"I'm sure they haven't practised as much as you have," Josh said. "You've been working really hard. You don't have anything to worry about."

"I hope you're right," Daniel said nervously.

Just then, a man in a denim jacket and jeans walked over. "You must be Daniel Granger," the man said.

"And you must be Mr Harlow," Daniel said. He stuck out his hand, and Mr Harlow shook it. "It's nice to meet you," Daniel added.

"The pleasure is mine," Mr Harlow said, smiling. "I'm always glad to meet NASCAR fans. Now, let's get started! Come on over here."

Daniel's dad and Josh went to watch from the stands. Daniel and the other contest winners introduced themselves.

Daniel had been right. The other boys were all in high school. He was the youngest boy there.

"The first thing you'll have you do is take a written test," Mr Harlow said.

Some of the older boys groaned. Mr Harlow chuckled. "Don't worry, guys, this isn't like school," he said. "This will help us work out how much you know about NASCAR and about racing."

Daniel and the other four essay contest winners spread out in the stands to take the test. It wasn't the most comfortable place to take a test, but it was definitely better than sitting in a classroom.

Daniel hadn't been expecting a written test. Still, the test was pretty easy. There wasn't a single question he couldn't answer.

Daniel knew that NASCAR had started from old bootleggers in the south. He knew that NASCAR stood for the National Association for Stock Car Auto Racing.

He also knew that the start of the NASCAR season actually began with the Daytona 500 in Daytona Beach, Florida. He would bet that a lot of people didn't know that.

Most people would probably assume that the racing season was like the football season. They might think that the Daytona 500 was kind of like the Super Bowl. But Daniel knew that it was held at the beginning of the racing season, not at the end.

Twenty minutes later, Daniel handed in his test. He was the first one done. He knew so much about NASCAR that he was sure that he could have answered even more questions.

While he waited for the other guys to finish their tests, he sat back, nervously tapping his feet.

He wanted to show those guys that he could work in a pit crew. He wanted to show them how quick he could be and how strong he was.

He might have been smaller and younger than the other boys, but he was ready for the challenge. He knew he could do it.

Soon, all the tests had been collected. It was time for the next trial.

Mr Harlow assigned each contestant a number. Daniel was given the number 3. For the next challenge, they had to pay attention to five race cars zooming around the track.

When the contestant's numbered car pulled into the stop, the contestant was supposed to hop over the wall and assist. The contestant would take his instructions from the pit crew already there.

Only seven people were allowed to work "over the wall." That was the spot where the race car slowed down and stopped for servicing.

The pit crew was responsible for refuelling the car, and for putting air in the tyres and changing them if needed. The pit crew also had to recognize any damage and fix it, if possible.

Sometimes the pit crew also helped the driver by making sure he had water to drink.

All these tasks took time, but the pit crew had to work very quickly. They only had fifteen seconds. After that, the car had to start moving again.

Daniel waited behind the wall. He watched as the cars zipped along. He looked at the number 3 car.

Finally, the number 3 car was slowing down! Now was his chance!

Daniel flung himself over the wall.

CHAPTER 5

SHOW YOUR STUFF

Daniel couldn't believe he was standing next to an actual race car. Of course, it probably wasn't like the official cars that had to pass qualifying races to enter a big NASCAR race. But he was as close as he had ever got to one!

Daniel was surprised when one of the pit crew members threw him a helmet and a pair of gloves.

"Safety first!" the man said.

Daniel put everything on as quickly as possible. *Am I being timed for getting dressed, too?* he wondered nervously.

Then he flew into action. Before he knew it, he was pumping air into tyres. He was washing windshields. He was helping to secure lug nuts.

Daniel could feel the blood rushing through his veins. His hands didn't shake at all as they handled the equipment.

The equipment wasn't exactly like what he'd practised on at home. How could it be? He'd practised on a normal car, and this was a race car. But the equipment still felt right in his hands.

Daniel's hands seemed to move all on their own. It was as if he'd been working in a pit crew forever.

He loved every minute of it – from the smell of the oil and grease to the feel of the warmth of the race car. The six other crew members did their jobs quickly. Everything worked together perfectly, down to the last lug nut.

Soon, the car was once again ready to roll. Daniel was tired, but thrilled. Working on the race car had been one of the best moments of his life.

As he stood there, catching his breath, Daniel watched the number 3 car ease down the track. The car slowed and stopped.

Busy in the pit crew, Daniel hadn't noticed the car's driver. Daniel had been too focused on the car. Now he watched as a familiar form emerged.

It was Jimmy Turner.

Jimmy Turner was a master race car driver. He had won several Daytona 500 races. He even starred in a few TV adverts. Jimmy Turner was a king of the racetrack. And he was one of Daniel's biggest idols.

Jimmy Turner waved at Daniel. "Come over here!" he called.

Daniel's hands began to sweat. He placed his gloves and helmet on the wall. Then he walked over to Jimmy.

"Good work, kid!" Jimmy said. "Was that really your first pit crew?"

Daniel gulped. "Um, yes. I mean, I practised with my dad in our garage," he added.

Jimmy laughed. "In your garage?" he asked.

"That's right," Daniel said. "But it doesn't really prepare you for the real thing."

"Not exactly," Jimmy said. "Even so, I think you did a great job."

"Really?" Daniel asked. He smiled.

"I'll talk to Mr Harlow, but I'd like to have you on my crew at least once this year," Jimmy told him. "What do you say?"

"What do I say?" Daniel said. What could he say? "I'd love it!"

CHAPTER 6

HARDER THAN BEFORE

Daniel brought Jimmy over to meet his dad and Josh. Daniel's father reached out to shake hands with the race car driver.

"It's a pleasure to meet you," Dad said. "Daniel and I have spent many hours watching you race."

"Thanks," Jimmy said, smiling. "It was a pleasure to have your son on my crew today."

"He's a hard worker," Dad said.

"Mr Turner asked me to work on his pit crew," Daniel told his dad.

Jimmy nodded. "Your son did a great job today," he said, "but we still have a way to go."

"You mean another test?" asked Daniel.

"Well, we don't let just anyone work in the pit crew," Jimmy explained. "Besides passing timed tests, each person has to get along with the rest of the crew. And they have to be very hard workers."

Jimmy paused. Then he went on, "The job isn't easy. Lots of people work hard to get here."

"I know Daniel would work hard, like everyone else," Dad said.

Jimmy nodded. "He's already shown that he has the ability," he said. "Now we have to see how well he'll be able to work with the team."

Jimmy arranged for Daniel to work with the pit crew for the next few Saturdays. Saturday races were usually qualifying races for the drivers. The big events were held on Sundays.

Daniel looked forward to every weekend. He loved the rush of the race cars zooming by. He loved the way the crew worked together so the car ran smoothly.

Daniel wasn't allowed to work over the wall during the races. But he still helped the pit crew. Instead of jumping over the wall, he'd stand on top of it. That way, he could pass down supplies that the race car driver and the crew needed.

Daniel quickly became part of the team. One of the jobs he always did was wiping down the tyres. The tyres needed to be cleaned off when they got covered in too much gunk. From his perch on the wall, Daniel reached down with a long-handled broom. He brushed the gunk off the tyres.

He was also a big help to the driver. He found a bucket and attached it to a broom handle. He filled the bucket with water bottles.

From the wall, Daniel reached the bucket toward Jimmy. Then all Jimmy had to do was lean over and grab the bottles.

The heat, the noise, the crowd! Daniel loved it. He didn't think there was any better place to spend a Saturday than a busy racetrack.

Then one Saturday, Jimmy walked over to Daniel after the race.

"Daniel, can you work the pit crew tomorrow?" Jimmy asked.

Daniel's mouth dropped open. He couldn't believe it. "Really?" he asked. "During the real race?"

Jimmy nodded. "I think you're ready," he said. "Now, let's go and find you a pit crew suit."

CHAPTER 7

THE WALL

Daniel could barely sleep that night. He was too busy thinking about brushing tyres and tightening lug nuts.

He got to the track early on Sunday morning. His dad and Josh headed towards the stands to watch the race.

Because of Daniel's age and his size, he still wasn't allowed to work over the wall. He'd be working on the wall, like he did during the qualifying races.

He was disappointed. At the same time, he also knew he was as close as he'd possibly get to a real NASCAR race.

As Daniel slipped his safety suit on, Jimmy walked up.

"The race is about to start," Jimmy said. "Do you think you're ready for your big debut?"

"Yes, sir. I wish I could work over the wall with the pit crew," Daniel said. "But I know I'm safer on the wall."

"No one's ever put someone your age over the wall before," Jimmy explained. "So let's see how you do on the wall first."

"Okay," Daniel said. "Good luck out there today!"

Jimmy walked away. Then Daniel started setting up.

He got his tools ready for the race. His giant broom was ready to wipe down the tyres. The bucket was full of water bottles to pass to the driver.

Soon, the race was about to begin. The crowd was getting louder and rowdier.

Daniel climbed onto the pit crew wall. He dangled his feet over the side. Within seconds, the race began.

Daniel kicked his heels against the pit crew wall as he watched the race. The cars zoomed around the track.

He kept his eyes on Jimmy's green and white car, the one with number 3 painted on the side in black paint. All of a sudden, the car quickly edged out of the pack of dozens of cars.

Jimmy Turner was making a move!

Daniel held his breath. In the audience, people started pointing to Jimmy Turner's race car.

Daniel checked his watch. He glanced at the giant wall clock near the pit crew station.

It was almost time for Jimmy Turner to pull over. His tyres needed air and rubbing down. Parts had to be checked.

And Jimmy was probably hot – really hot – inside his race car. Daniel knew that the temperature inside a race car could be more than 100 degrees. Jimmy would need a drink of cold water as soon as he pulled into the pit.

Daniel watched as the green and white car slowed down. It neared the pit. It slid to a stop behind the wall.

Daniel got ready to stand up. He was prepared.

The first thing he'd do would be to lean over and run his broom across the surface of the car's dirty tyres.

Daniel started to get to his feet. Then, suddenly, everything went wrong.

CHAPTER 8

CAR BONNETS

In all the weeks Daniel had worked with the pit crew, he'd never seen a car leave the track and drive into the wall. The movement was completely unexpected.

One minute, Daniel had been standing on the wall. The next moment, the wall shook and he was airborne.

Then his feet slammed into the bonnet of the race car.

Daniel's entire body seemed to rattle and grind. The race car shook like mad beneath him.

Somehow, Daniel still managed to hold onto the broom and the bottle of ice water. He didn't drop anything.

Jimmy flung himself out of the car. "What do you think you're doing?" he shouted up at Daniel.

Daniel felt like he'd been punched in the gut. He'd hit the car really hard. He couldn't seem to catch his breath.

"I fell," Daniel said.

"That's pretty obvious," Jimmy said.

The pit crew had gone into emergency mode. Daniel's father came jogging up. Josh was right behind him. They had prime seats in the infield.

Dad and Josh had seen everything – from Daniel climbing the wall to Daniel nearly getting crushed by the race car. Dad looked really worried.

Daniel was glad he was wearing the safety suit. If it hadn't been for all of the extra padding, he was sure his body would be in a million pieces.

"I hope I didn't smash up the car too much," he said to Mark, the head of the pit crew.

"Let's get you up off that bonnet and see what damage was done – to you and the car," Mark replied. "With luck, both of you will be okay. That was quite a fall you just had."

Dad reached out his hands. He helped Daniel get off the bonnet.

Daniel turned to look at the car. The bonnet still seemed sturdy. There weren't any dents or bumps or cracks. That was good news.

Daniel's back hurt, but the car was fine. But Jimmy still looked upset. His face was red, and he wouldn't look at Daniel.

Suddenly, a stretcher appeared at the side of the race car. Daniel heard a cheer go up in the grandstands and in the infield. He realized that the audience was cheering for him. They were cheering because Daniel was able to move.

Daniel let his father and Josh help him onto the stretcher. Daniel was afraid to look at the pit crew. He was mostly afraid to look at Jimmy. They had all put so much faith in him, despite his age and his size. He knew he had let them down.

Daniel leaned back on the stretcher. He watched as the scenery changed overhead. Two ambulance drivers lifted him into the ambulance. Daniel listened as the cheering and whistling continued.

Then the ambulance doors slammed shut. Everything was quiet as he was taken to the hospital.

CHAPTER 9

IN THE HOSPITAL

Dad and Josh met the ambulance at the hospital. After the ambulance drivers rolled Daniel into the building, Dad leaned over to give him a hug. Then he thought better of it. Daniel was all bashed and bruised, after all. A hug would hurt him more than help.

Even the ride on the stretcher was painful. The stretcher bounced along the winding hospital corridors.

Daniel was certain he'd need X-rays or something. The doctors would have to make sure he hadn't broken anything too seriously.

Daniel wiggled his arms and legs. Everything seemed to be working. Sweat began to bead on his forehead. He was starting to feel uncomfortable and hot in his safety suit.

The ambulance drivers wheeled Daniel into the emergency room. They brought him to an empty bed.

Daniel watched as Dad pulled the privacy curtain around his bed. There was a small TV nearby, tuned to the NASCAR race.

"I still don't understand how you managed to get yourself knocked off the wall," Dad said.

Daniel wanted to shrug, but it hurt too much. The pain was getting to be unbearable.

"I guess a real race is very different from working with the crew at a practice race," Daniel said. "I should have practised falling," he added.

Just then, a bunch of doctors and nurses marched over to Daniel's bed. One of the doctors slid a heartbeat monitor over Daniel's arm.

The other doctors took his temperature and checked his blood pressure. Everything seemed normal.

"I think you just need to rest," one of the nurses said. "And we'll get you out of this suit and into something a little more comfortable."

Daniel actually wanted to keep wearing his safety suit. As long as he had it on, he still felt like he was part of the pit crew.

If he changed into the hospital clothes, he'd have to admit that he'd messed things up. He'd let Jimmy down.

Just then, the privacy curtain was pushed aside. Daniel couldn't believe it when he saw the familiar face. Jimmy Turner walked up to his bed.

"What are you doing here?" Daniel asked, shocked. "Shouldn't you be finishing the race right now?"

"I had to make sure you were okay," Jimmy explained. "I can't let a member of my team go to the hospital without checking on them," he added. "I was worried about you."

Daniel looked away from Jimmy. "I suppose I'm not part of the team anymore," Daniel said sadly. "After what happened today, I mean."

Jimmy frowned. "Who says? It's my decision who works on my team," he told Daniel. "Now that we both know what to expect, we'll be more careful. You'll wear more safety gear, for one thing. And we'll keep you behind the wall. You'll get special equipment so you can still help out, but you'll be safer that way. I don't want to lose one of the hardest-working members of my team."

"Really?" Daniel asked happily. "I can keep working on the crew?" He looked over at his dad.

"If we can make sure you're safe, I don't see a problem," Dad said.

Daniel smiled. "Yes!" he said. "We can go over all the safety stuff before I work another race."

"Speaking of races, today's is only half over," Jimmy said. "Let's watch the rest. Let's see which bucket of bolts actually wins!"

Daniel laughed. The pain he'd felt almost disappeared. He and Jimmy sat back and watched the rest of the race.

ABOUT THE AUTHOR

Lisa Trumbauer is the best-selling author of *A Practical Guide to Dragons*. In addition, she has written about 300 other books for children, including mystery novels, picture books, and non-fiction books on just about every topic under the Sun (including the Sun!).

ABOUT THE ILLUSTRATOR

When Sean Tiffany was growing up, he lived on a small island. Every day, he had to take a boat to get to school. When Sean isn't working on his art, he works on a multimedia project called "OilCan Drive", which combines music and art. He has a pet cactus named Jim.

GLOSSARY

committee group of people who discuss things and make decisions for a larger group

competition person you are trying to beat in a contest

confidence strong belief in a person's abilities

contestant person who takes part in a contest

experienced made skillful from the practise of doing something

guarantee a promise that something will definitely happen

mechanics related to machines

WHO'S WHO IN THE
PIT CREW

A pit crew consists of a jackman, two tyre changers, two tire carriers, a gasman, and a catch can man. Here's a quick guide to who does what.

During tyre changes, the **jackman** lifts one side of the car with a hydraulic jack for tyre changes. After the first side is changed, the jackman must hurry around to the other side, carrying the 16-kilogram jack. He then jacks up that side.

The **tyre changers** use an airgun to loosen and tighten the lug nuts that hold on the tyres. There is a changer for the front tyres and one for the rear tyres.

The **tyre carriers** help the changers. They carry 34-kilogram tyres from behind the wall and put them on the car. The changers can then tighten the lug nuts.

The **gasman** is responsible for filling the car's fuel cell. He hoists a 36-kilogram petrol can up to the car to fill the cell. One or two petrol cans are used per pit stop, depending on how much fuel is needed.

The **catch can man** catches fuel when the tank is full. The catch can is shaped like a box. It has a valve that plugs in to the back of the car. When the tank is full, extra fuel flows out the valve and into the catch can. Then, the catch can man waves to let the driver know that the fuel cell is full.

DISCUSSION QUESTIONS

1. How do you think Daniel felt when he saw the other boys he had to compete against for a spot on the pit crew?

2. Why do you think the contest included a written exam? Why was it important for the contestants to know so much about NASCAR?

3. Do you think it was a good decision for Jimmy to leave the race at the end of the book?

WRITING PROMPTS

1. Daniel worked hard to earn a spot on the pit crew. Have you ever worked hard to achieve a goal? Write about your experience.

2. Have you ever injured yourself while participating in a sport or activity? Write about it.

3. Reread the first two pages of chapter seven. Think about what Jimmy was seeing from inside the car. Now rewrite the scene from his point of view.

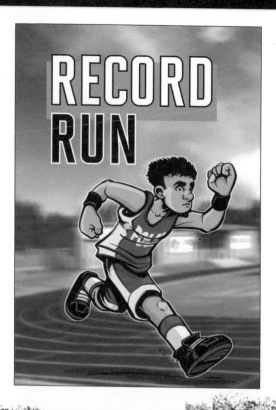

When harry thows a water balloon at the captain of the running team, he knows he better get away fast. He is finally caught, but the captain gives him an unexpected choice: get soaked, or join the team. But will Harry still find it fun to run if he isn't being chased?

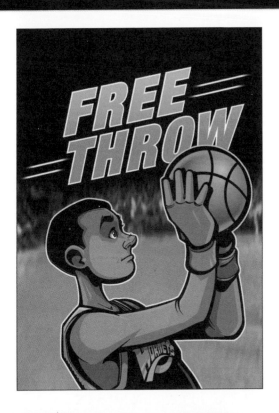

Theo is the tallest kid on his basketball team, so his coach decides to have him play centre instead of Jason. Theo thinks this is a lucky break, until Jason takes revenge. Will he ever be able to make a free thow with Jason breathing down his neck?

FIND OUT MORE

BOOKS

Amazing NASCAR Races, Jim Gigliotti (Crabtree Publishing, 2008)

Famous NASCAR Tracks, Jim Gigliotti (Crabtree Publishing, 2008)

Great NASCAR Champions, Jim Gigliotti (Crabtree Publishing, 2008)

Great NASCAR Teams, Jim Gigliotti (Crabtree Publishing, 2008)

The History of NASCAR, Jim Francis (Crabtree Publishing, 2008)

NASCAR, David Clayton (ticktock Media, 2008)

WEBSITES

www.nascar.com

Visit the official NASCAR website to find all the most up-to-date information about the sport.